MARVEL STUDIOS

SPIDER-MAN
No Way Home

Spider-Man's
Very Strange Day!

Words by Calliope Glass
Pictures by Andrew Kolb

Los Angeles
New York

Feeling a little cooped up, Spider-Man?

Starting to feel like everyone's out to get you?

That's because they are!

New plan: Never leave home again.

It's been a long week, what with your identity being revealed to the world . . .

. . . and you need some cheering up.

If after all that you're *still* in the spider-dumps . . .

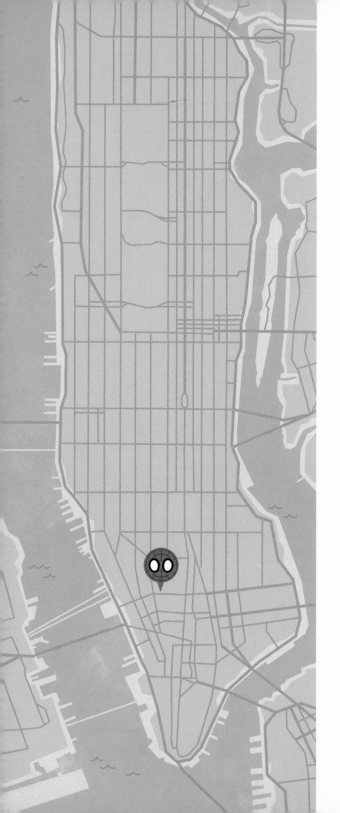

. . . then it's time for a field trip.

Something fun!

Something new!

Something kinda dangerous!

Hurry on down to . . .

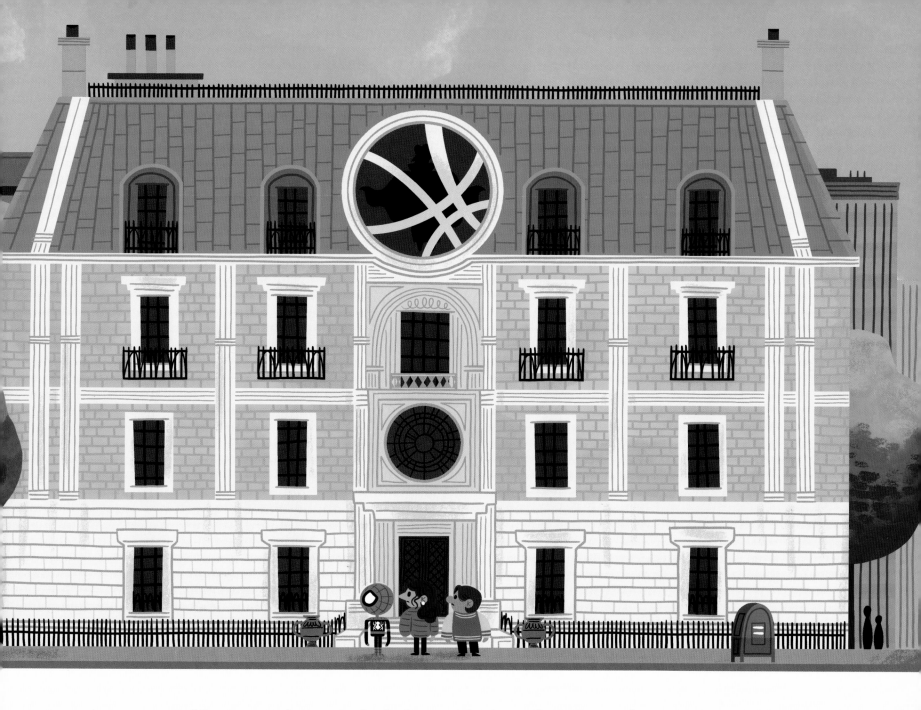

It's a mysterious, magical place and a home for crabby wizards, all rolled into one!

Get ready to look, listen, and learn!

The wise masters
of the Sanctum will
greet you . . .

. . . and the expert
staff can't wait to
broaden your horizons!

So come on in
and meet one of the masters . . .
DOCTOR STRANGE!
(Don't touch his coffee.)

Go on a tour of the
Sanctum, including . . .

THE MIRROR DIMENSION!

Stop by for an interactive experience that bends the laws of physics!
Is it thrilling, or is it terrifying? The answer is *yes*!

Next, be sure to check out THE UNDERCROFT!

Okay, it's pretty much just a dirty basement. But still! Try on a novelty mustache or silly beard, just for fun. They *mustache* you not to laugh. Get it?

Make friends with other visitors! Some of them are rats!

Not a rat person?

Perhaps a dance party will help! Study energy and magic . . .

. . . and take the time to let loose!

Fun fact! Strange's Sanctum is one of many on Earth ensuring the planet is safe.

Without them, the world would be vulnerable to all sorts of danger.

Isn't learning things neat?

SNOWBALL FIGHT!

Plus, the New York Sanctum has
awesome portals to other ecosystems.
Get to know all about climate diversity!

Enter a world of excitement and exploration! But also watch out for that open portal, Ned!

Oops, too late.
He'll be fine.
Probably.

In the meantime,
step on over to . . .

Look, listen, and learn about these ancient artifacts of the mystical world!
Please be sure to handle with care. Except that axe. Don't touch that.

Ancient artifacts are cool and all, but the best thing about the Sanctum Sanctorum? Unlimited beverages, of course! These neat collectible cups violate the laws of thermodynamics!

See, being **SpideR-MAN** isn't so bad.

In the end, what you really needed was a fun day with your friends, learning all about the mysteries of the world!

And even if you must face new troubles, you can always return to . . .

You're right where you're meant to be. Ah, home sweet spidey-home.

MARVEL

Designed by Catalina Castro

Printed in the United States of America

First Edition, November 2021 10 9 8 7 6 5 4 3 2 1

ISBN: 978-1-368-06999-1

FAC- 034274-21260

Library of Congress Control Number: 2021936533

Reinforced binding